This Makes Me Angry

DEALING WITH FEELINGS

by Courtney Carbone
illustrated by Hilli Kushnir

Random House New York

BEEP! BEEP! BEEP!
My alarm clock goes off.
It sounds like yelling.
I want to yell back.

My little brother, Jack,
bursts into my room.
He wants to play.
I want to sleep.

I go into the bathroom.
Jack made a huge mess!

I feel heat rising
inside of me.
It is not just
from the shower.

Dad makes pancakes
for breakfast.
I like the crispy ones,
but Jack eats them all!

Mom's tea kettle is
boiling hot.
My insides are
boiling, too.

We get to school.
My teacher asks
for our homework.
I pull mine out.

Oh no!
My paper is covered
in crayon.
It is all Jack's fault.

I have to do the work
all over again!

My chest feels tight.
It stays that way
all morning.

Soon it is lunchtime.
I can't get my milk open.
I feel like I am going
to explode.

I rip the carton open.
It goes everywhere!

My friends laugh.
They think
it is funny.

I try to stay calm.
It does not work.
I yell at them instead.

A teacher sends me
to the principal.
Now I feel awful.

My face is hot.
My clothes are sticky.
I just want to go home.

The principal asks
what happened.

I start to cry.
I tell her everything.
She listens calmly.

The principal hands me
a small notebook.

She tells me
I can use the book
to draw how I feel.

I think about
all the bad things
that happened today.

What am I feeling?
I am feeling ANGRY.

I take a deep breath.
I draw everything
I feel in the book.

The pictures are
actually kind of funny.
I am not as angry now.

I go back to class.
I see the kids
from lunch.

I tell them I am sorry.
They apologize, too.
I feel a lot better.

I tell my family
about the book
when I get home.

ack wants to draw, too.
give him the book.
le starts to scribble
n my drawings.

Jack draws a picture
of us holding hands.
I give him a hug.
All my anger melts away.

Today started out
as a bad day.
But it turned into
a very good one.

For anyone having a bad day, that they may turn it around

—C.B.C.

To Liam and Aya, for all things broken, spilled, torn, lost, scattered, forgotten, and ruined that made me momentarily ANGRY

—H.K.

 Published in the United States by Random House Children's Books, a division of Penguin Random House LLC, New York. Originally published by Rodale Kids, an imprint of Random House Children's Books, a division of Penguin Random House LLC, New York, in 2018.

Step into Reading, Random House, and the Random House colophon are registered trademarks of Penguin Random House LLC.

Visit us on the Web!
rhcbooks.com

Educators and librarians, for a variety of teaching tools, visit us at
RHTeachersLibrarians.com

The Library of Congress has cataloged the hardcover edition of this work as follows:
ISBN 978-0-593-56487-5 (trade) — ISBN 978-0-593-56488-2 (lib. bdg.) —
ISBN 978-0-593-56489-9 (ebook)

Printed in the United States of America
10 9 8 7 6 5 4 3 2 1

This book has been officially leveled by using the F&P Text Level Gradient™ Leveling System.